A Note to Parents

Read to your child...

★ Reading aloud is one of the best ways to develop your child's love of reading. Read together at least 20 minutes each day.

★ Laughter is contagious! Read with feeling. Show your child that reading is fun.

★ Take time to answer questions your child may have about the story. Linger over pages that interest your child.

...and your child will read to you.

★ Do not correct every word your child misreads. Instead, say, "Does that make sense? Let's try it again."

★ Praise your child as he progresses. Your encouraging words will build his confidence.

You can help your Level 2 reader.

★ Keep the reading experience interactive. Read part of a sentence, then ask your child to add the missing word.

★ Read the first part of a story. Then ask, "What's going to happen next?"

★ Give clues to new words. Say, "This word begins with *b* and ends in *ake*, like *rake*, *take*, *lake*."

★ Ask your child to retell the story using her own words.

★ Use the five *W*s: WHO is the story about? WHAT happens? WHERE and WHEN does the story take place? WHY does it turn out the way it does?

Most of all, enjoy your reading time together!

**—Bernice Cullinan, Ph.D.,
Professor of Reading, New York University**

Published by Reader's Digest Children's Books
Reader's Digest Road, Pleasantville, NY U.S.A. 10570-7000 and
Reader's Digest Children's Publishing Limited,
The Ice House, 124-126 Walcot Street, Bath UK BA1 5BG
Copyright © 2000 Reader's Digest Children's Publishing, Inc.
All rights reserved. Reader's Digest Children's Books is a trademark and
Reader's Digest and All-Star Readers are registered trademarks of
The Reader's Digest Association, Inc. Fisher-Price trademarks are used
under license from Fisher-Price, Inc., a subsidiary of
Mattel, Inc., East Aurora, NY 14052 U.S.A.
©2000 Mattel, Inc. All Rights Reserved.
Printed in Hong Kong.
10 9 8 7 6

Library of Congress Cataloging-in-Publication Data

Hood, Susan.
    Scaredy-cat sleepover / by Susan Hood ; illustrated by Nadine Bernard Westcott.
        p. cm. — (All-star readers. Level 2)
    Summary: A girl's sleepover party turns scary when her little sisters are excluded.
    ISBN 1-57584-386-2 (alk. paper)
    [1. Sleepovers Fiction. 2. Parties Fiction. 3. Stories in rhyme.]
    I. Westcott, Nadine Bernard, ill. II. Title. III Series.
    PZ8.3.H7577Sc 2000   [E]—dc21   99-34715

Scaredy-Cat Sleepover

by Susan Hood
illustrated by Nadine Bernard Westcott

All-Star Readers

Reader's Digest Children's Books™
Pleasantville, New York • Montréal, Québec

Ann called Amy,
Chris, and Marty.
"Can you come
to my birthday party?

We'll sleep outside
and have some cake.
We'll talk and giggle
and stay awake!"

"Can we come, too?"
her sisters said.

"No way!" said Ann.
"You'll be in bed!

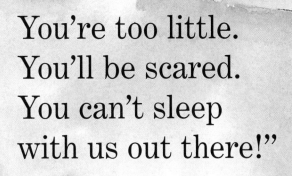

You're too little.
You'll be scared.
You can't sleep
with us out there!"

The big girls came.
They teased the twins.

"Bye, scaredy cats!"
they said with grins.

The big girls danced

and gobbled cake.

They talked and giggled

and stayed awake.

Ann told her friends
a spooky tale.

Their eyes grew wide.
Their cheeks grew pale.

Then something snapped!
Someone said, "Eek!"

The girls all froze.
What was that creak?

They heard a CRASH!
"Help! HELP!" cried Ann.

The girls all screamed
and then they ran.

They ran inside
and slammed the door.

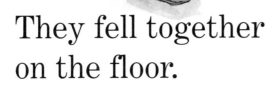

They fell together
on the floor.

Ann giggled first.
Chris giggled back.

"Boy, that was close!
Let's have a snack."

Then something tapped!
And something creaked!
The girls all froze . . .

... and then they shrieked!

The girls all screamed
and then they ran.

"Let's get my dad!
He'll help!" cried Ann.

Ann's dad got up
and went outside.

The girls were pale.
Their eyes were wide.

Outside they found
two giggling twins.

"Hi, scaredy cats!"
they said with grins.

Words are fun!

Here are some simple activities you can do with a pencil, crayons, and a sheet of paper. You'll find the answers at the bottom of the page.

———— ★ ————

1. Big words often have little words inside them. Cover some of the letters of each word with your fingers to see what little words you can find.

scared	**heard**
teased	**screamed**
someone	**something**

2. Which word is closest in meaning to the word on the left?

giggle (cough, stretch, laugh)

spooky (scary, funny, wild)

shriek (shine, scream, drive)

grin (paste, draw, smile)

little (small, great, friendly)

3. Match the words that are opposites:

inside	**brave**
awake	**frown**
little	**outside**
grin	**asleep**
scared	**big**

4. What happened next? Put the sentences below in the order things occurred in the story.

a. **Ann told a spooky tale.**

b. **The twins called Ann and her friends scaredy-cats.**

c. **The big girls got scared.**

d. **The big girls teased the twins.**

e. **Ann's dad helped the girls.**